To Mum and Dad

Kane/Miller Book Publishers, Inc.
First American Edition 2008
by Kane/Miller Book Publishers, Inc.
La Jolla, California

First published by Penguin Group (Australia), a division of
Pearson Australia Group Pty Ltd., 2007
Copyright © Judy Horacek, 2007

Library of Congress Control Number: 2008920672
Printed and bound in China
1 2 3 4 5 6 7 8 9 10

ISBN: 978-1-933605-80-7

The story of GROWL

Judy Horacek

Kane/Miller
BOOK PUBLISHERS

This is Growl.

Growl is a little monster.

She lives alone in a castle at the end of Eucalyptus Drive.

Growl likes to hop ...

and skip ...

and jump ...

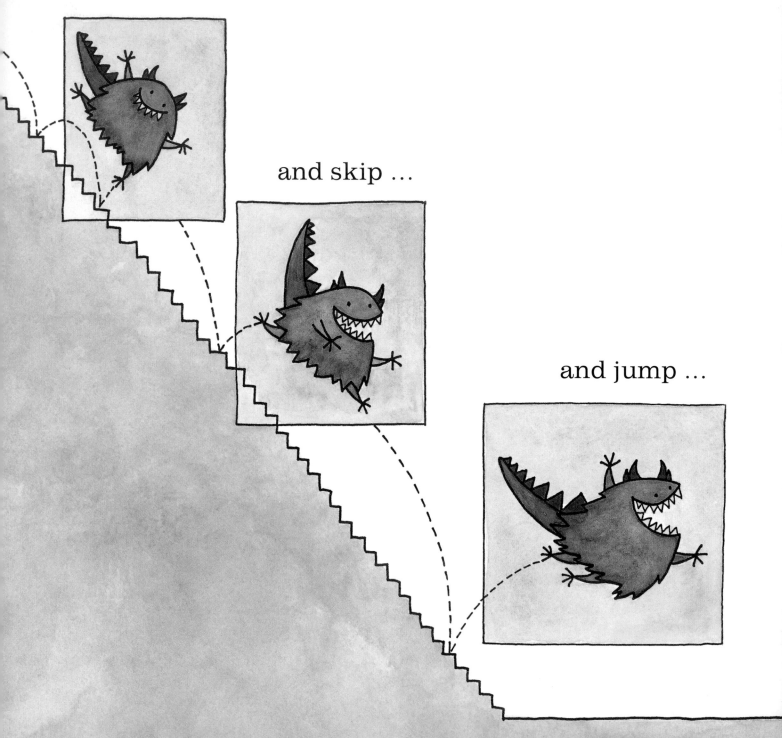

and run around her garden.

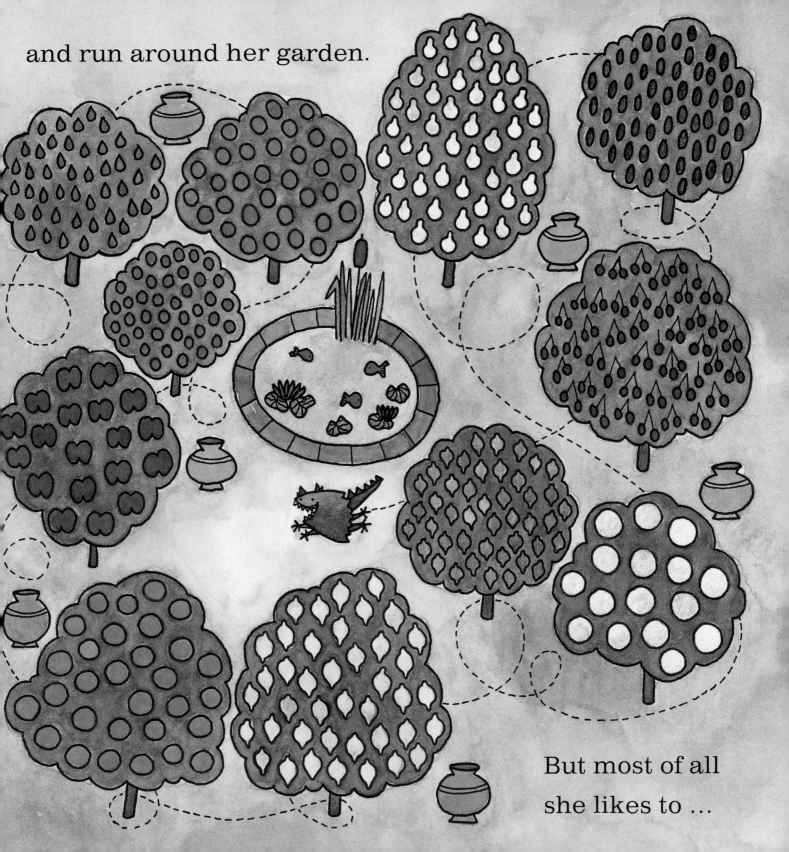

But most of all
she likes to …

She growls in the morning. She growls in the afternoon. She growls the whole day, right up until bedtime.

She growls all through the week,
and on Sundays she sings a little song,

One day Growl found herself sneaking across
her garden towards the neighbors' fence.
She climbed up and ...

"This has gone far enough!" said the first neighbor.

"If we've told you once, we've told you a thousand times!" said the second neighbor.

"It's bad enough living next door to a little monster, but we will not have you growling at us at afternoon teatime," said both the neighbors together.

The neighbors telephoned the police, who made up a special rule. A policeman came to put up a sign.

"This means you," he said to Growl.

No growling!

Growl was the saddest she'd ever been.

She tried to hop and skip and jump, but it was no good. She tried to run around her garden, but running is hard when you're trying not to cry.

The days seemed
to go on forever ...

and at night she couldn't sleep.

On Sunday she sang very softly to herself,

Late one night Growl was looking out her window. She saw a strange man creeping across the neighbors' garden.

Before Growl knew what she was doing
she opened her mouth and ...

GROWL!

The strange man ran away as fast as he could.

The noise woke the neighbors and
they came running out of their house.

"You have scared away the robber!"
said the first neighbor.

"And saved our afternoon tea set!"
said the second neighbor.

"Maybe your growling isn't so
bad after all," said both the
neighbors together.

When the sun came up, the neighbors rang the police to say that the special NO GROWLING rule was no longer necessary.

"Good," said the policeman. "It was much too quiet in your neighborhood."

Growl could growl again!

Growl growled for the rest of the morning and into the afternoon. And even though it wasn't Sunday, she sang her old song,

But she added a new line,

And when afternoon tea is over in Eucalyptus Drive …

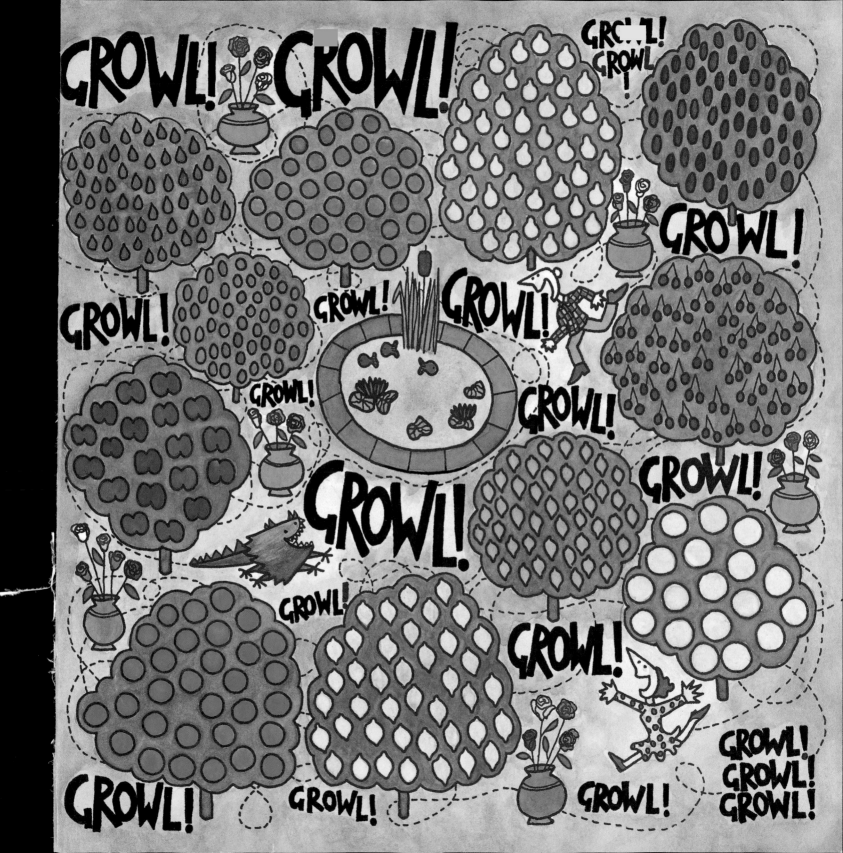